This book belongs to:

_____

To Bella – Sweet dreams.

Also by Jessica Meserve:

SMALL

CAN ANYBODY HEAR ME?

First published in Great Britain in 2009 by Andersen Press Ltd., 20 Vauxhall Bridge Road, London SW1V 2SA.
This paperback edition first published in 2010 by Andersen Press Ltd.
Published in Australia by Random House Australia Pty., Level 3, 100 Pacific Highway, North Sydney, NSW 2060.
Copyright © Jessica Meserve, 2009. The rights of Jessica Meserve to be identified as the author and illustrator of this
work have been asserted by her in accordance with the Copyright, Designs and Patents Act, 1988.
All rights reserved. Colour separated in Switzerland by Photolitho AG, Zürich.
Printed and bound in Singapore by Tien Wah Press.
10   9   8   7   6   5   4   3   2   1
British Library Cataloguing in Publication Data available.
ISBN 978 1 84270 943 6
This book has been printed on acid-free paper

Bedtime Without ARTHUR

Jessica Meserve

ANDERSEN PRESS

Bella has a bear.
A very special bear called Arthur.

He is as brave as a knight.
He is as strong as ten elephants.

And he does karate.

When Bella sleeps,

Arthur  is BUSY.

He guards the bed and keeps away monsters that come sneaking from the shadows.

Safe in her bed,
Bella dreams
of her favourite things,
like rainbows
and rainforests.

One morning, Arthur was worn out from so much karate.

Bella made him his favourite breakfast of toast and honey, and then tucked him up snug in bed.

That evening, when the
moon had risen full and
white, Bella went to her
room to give
Arthur a slice of
pizza for supper.

Bella pulled
back the quilt
and...

...yowled,

"Arthur!"

He
was
gone.

Bella **searched**

and **searched.**

Bella's mum looked upstairs.
Bella's dad looked downstairs.
Bella's brother, Finley,
looked worried.

None of them could find Arthur
ANYWHERE.

Mum said, "We'll find him tomorrow."

Dad said, "He'll turn up."

Finley said, "Sorry."

But Bella didn't believe them.
Her lip trembled as she
climbed into bed.

Bella couldn't sleep.
She was sure there were
MONSTERS watching and waiting.

Bella squeezed her eyes tight shut.
She fell asleep dreaming of

FIRE-BREATHING DRAGONS,
SLUGS
and grizzly bears.

In the morning, Bella
was exhausted.

She couldn't juggle.

Even the ice cream didn't cheer her up.

And at bedtime there
was still
no sign
of Arthur.

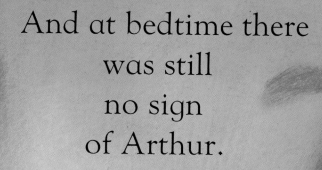

The wind began to

blow and howl.

Bella woke with a start.

She saw things
looming and
scratching at
the glass.

Bella leapt out of bed and ran as fast
as she could across the hallway
into her brother's room.

Finley was sound asleep.
Bella began climbing
into his cot.

Peeking from under the blanket, she
saw the tip of a soft, furry nose.

It was Arthur!

Bella was **so** happy to see him . . .

. . . but she was
very angry with her
brother for taking him.

She grabbed Arthur and started back to her room.

Left all alone, Finley was afraid.
"Monsters!" he cried.
Bella pretended not to listen.

"Serves him right," she thought
as she reached the door.

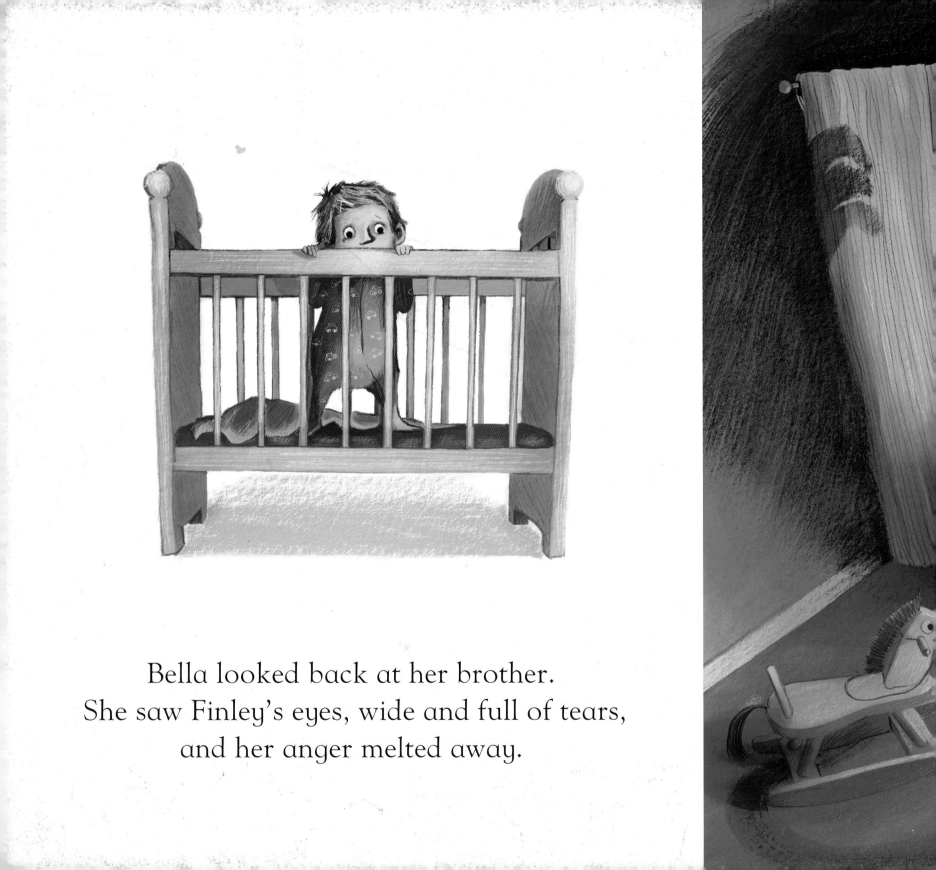

Bella looked back at her brother.
She saw Finley's eyes, wide and full of tears,
and her anger melted away.

Bella realised that Finley needed
Arthur more than she did. Finley
wasn't nearly as strong and brave
as she was.

Bella took Arthur back to
Finley and tucked them
both up in bed.
"Don't be scared, Finley, Arthur
will look after you."

Bella felt braver and
braver with each
step she took back
to her room.

When at last she climbed into bed, Bella felt as brave as a knight. All the monsters shook with fear and fizzled into nothing.

That night Bella slept long and deep and dreamt of all her favourite things.

And so did Finley.

Also by Jessica Meserve

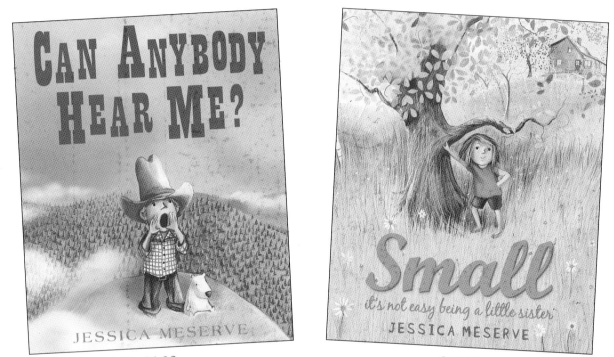

9781842708361 £5.99

9781842706091 £5.99

'Her warm, expressive and funny illustrations
hold a lot of child appeal.'

CHILDREN'S BOOKSELLER